Matzah Ball Soup

JOAN ROTHENBERG

HYPERION BOOKS FOR CHILDREN

New York

ROBIN AND RHEA AND HALEY

Library of Congress
Cataloging-in-Publication data
Rothenberg, Joan.
Matzah ball soup / Joan Rothenberg.
p.   cm.
Summary: Rosie discovers why there are
always four different kinds of matzah balls in the
Passover matzah ball soup.
ISBN 0-7868-0202-2 (trade)-
ISBN 0-7868-2170-1 (library)
[1. Passover-Fiction. 2. Jews-United States-
Fiction. 3. Food-Fiction.] I. Title.
PZ7.R7425Mat 1996
[E]-dc20   95-24432

AUNTIE LORETTA AND COUSIN BERTSIE

LOVE TO COUSIN JUDITH SUSAN, PHD AND LITTLE CUZ DALE ANN

"Come here, Rosie Posie, I need some pinches," said Grandma.

"Okay, Grandma, where do you want them?" Rosie giggled.

She began giving Grandma little pinches.

"Now, now, don't be silly," Grandma chuckled. "I need two pinches of ginger and three pinches of paprika, right here in this bowl."

Rosie watched as Grandma added five handfuls of matzah meal. "How do you know how much to put in?" she asked.

"I know by how it feels," said Grandma. "When it feels right, I've got enough."

"Grandma, this whole kitchen is full of matzah balls," said Rosie. "I bet we have enough for a hundred Seders."

"Oh, no, Rosie Posie, there's not nearly enough," said Grandma. "The entire family will be here for the Passover Seder and some friends and neighbors, too. So many people, so many bowls of chicken soup! And you know, there must be four matzah balls in every bowl."

"Why?" asked Rosie.

"Because it's tradition," Grandma replied.

"What's tradition?" asked Rosie.

"A tradition is something we do because we've done it for a long time," Grandma explained. "Haven't I ever told you about my Tanta Tee's first Passover in America?"

"No, Grandma," replied Rosie.

"When I was just about your age, my Tanta Tee left her home in Hungary and came to America to live with us," Grandma began.

"She missed her brother, my uncle Russell, and her sisters, my mama, and my Tantas Gizella and Gabi. Most of all, she came to America to be free."

"Was she a slave like when we were in Egypt?" asked Rosie.

"No, Rosie, Tanta Tee wasn't a slave," said Grandma, "but her home was not a safe place for Jews to live."

"But what does she have to do with four matzah balls in our soup?" asked Rosie.

"When it came time for Passover, Tanta Tee decided that she should be the one to make the matzah balls for the chicken soup.

"'I am the oldest,' she said, 'and I made the tastiest matzah balls in all of Budapest!'

"'They certainly are the spiciest,' said Tanta Gizella, 'but I think the best matzah ball is the one that complements the flavor of the soup. Mine are so delicate, you hardly know they're there at all.'

"'If you don't know they're there, why bother making them?' asked Tanta Gabi. 'Everyone knows that the best matzah ball is one you can really sink your teeth into.'

"'Your matzah balls are real sinkers, that's for sure,' declared my mama. 'Mine are so fluffy, you could eat a dozen and never feel full.'"

"'*Humph!!*' scoffed Tanta Tee.

"'The audacity!' snapped Tanta Gizella.

"'How rude,' scolded Tanta Gabi.

"'*Gottenyu!* Enough already!' protested Uncle Russell. 'How can we celebrate Tee's first Passover in America with all of this quarreling and kvetching? Let's settle this squabble fair and square. Each of you will make your matzah balls and the whole family will decide which one is best.'"

"So the day before the Passover Seder, we began making matzah balls.

"Tanta Gabi and Tanta Gizella spent hours fussing over their special recipes. Tanta Gabi kept tasting as she cooked to make sure she didn't make any mistakes. Tanta Gizella ran out of matzah meal and had to make some more out of big pieces of matzah.

"Mama and Tanta Tee had to share my mama's kitchen, so it took them twice as long to make their matzah balls. Mama was still making hers long after the rest of us had gone to bed."

"By the time sundown came and the Seder celebration began, all of the sisters were very nervous and so tired they could hardly see straight. They hovered over the batches of matzah balls like mother hens. But before the soup could be served, we had to read from the Haggadah.

"We said the blessings and drank the wine and dipped the parsley into the saltwater, just as we did every year.

"Then it came time for my little brother, Sam, to ask the Four Questions for the very first time. I always liked the one about leaning on pillows at the dinner table. Tanta Gabi couldn't sit still, so her pillow kept falling off her chair."

"When we sang about the Four Children, my cousin Sophie insisted upon being the Wise Child and I got stuck being the Wicked one. We heard about how we were freed from slavery in Egypt and then we tasted the bitter herbs.

"The spicy horseradish burned Tanta Gizella's tongue and tickled her nose. She sneezed and choked and tears poured down her cheeks. 'This horseradish is almost as spicy as Tee's matzah balls,' she muttered under her breath.

"'I heard that!' snapped Tanta Tee.

"Tanta Gabi leaned over and retrieved her fallen pillow.

"'Now, ladies,' Uncle Russell said. 'We are all looking forward to sampling those magnificent matzah balls of yours, but if you don't calm down, we won't be eating dinner until midnight!'"

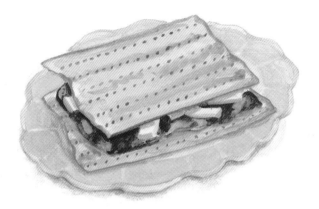

"So we tasted the sweet *charoset* and we made it into a sandwich with the bitter herbs and the matzah.

"'The matzah balls are cooking too long!' my mama cried. She jumped up and ran from the table.

"'I give up!' Uncle Russell threw up his hands. 'So go *already*, bring out the soup.'"

"We waited anxiously as the soup was brought to the table. You could have heard a pin drop when Uncle Russell lifted his spoon and tasted the first matzah ball. He motioned for all of us to do the same. Choosing the

best matzah ball was not going to be easy. Uncle Nathan insisted that he couldn't make his choice until he had eaten a whole dozen."

"Who won the contest?" asked Rosie. "I bet it was your mama, wasn't it?"

"We ate our soup without saying a word. There were sniffs, some slurps, and a few coughs. Cousin Edith took a big bite of one matzah ball, turned red, and drank a whole glass of water. Uncle Nathan just kept asking for more."

"But WHO WON?" Rosie demanded.

"While we did the tasting, the nervous sisters stood around the table, crossing their fingers and watching us eat," said Grandma.

"No one dared say anything."

"Uncle Russell looked at all of us, and we looked at each other. He wiped his mouth and slowly rose from his chair. 'There is absolutely no contest,' he announced.

"The sisters held their breath.

" 'We couldn't possibly eat our chicken soup on Passover without each one of these remarkable matzah balls!' he concluded."

"They all won!" cheered Rosie. "That's why we have four different matzah balls in our soup, right?"

"That's right," answered Grandma. She wiped her hands on her apron. "Let me see your hands, Rosie Posie," she said.

"Hmmm, just right. Please put a handful of parsley and another of matzah meal into this bowl."

"Sure," said Rose. "But why did you have to see my hand first?"

"This is Mama's recipe," said Grandma. "I was just your age when Mama let me put in the parsley and the last handful of matzah meal. Your handfuls will be just right."

"Grandma, your mama and the tantas aren't alive anymore," said Rosie. "How come we still have to put the four matzah balls in the chicken soup?"

"That's tradition, Rosie Posie! Everyone expects them to be there," Grandma answered. "And for me, when I see the four matzah balls in my bowl, it feels as though my mama and the tantas are at the Seder with us."

"And now I'm making the matzah balls, too," said Rosie. "So when I eat my chicken soup, I can think about you!"

She gave Grandma a big hug and a whole lot of pinches, just for good measure.

Mama's Matzah Balls

You'll need:
4 tablespoons chicken fat
  (or oil or shortening)
1/4 teaspoon nutmeg
1/4 teaspoon ginger
1 teaspoon salt

1/4 teaspoon pepper
4 eggs
8 tablespoons seltzer water
1 1/4 cups matzah meal
chopped parsley (to taste)

1. Blend fat, ginger, nutmeg, salt, and pepper.
2. In a separate bowl, beat eggs slightly.
3. Add fat mixture, seltzer, parsley, and matzah meal to the eggs and mix thoroughly.
4. Chill for several hours or overnight.
5. Form mixture into walnut-sized balls and cook covered in boiling salted water for 50–60 minutes. (If batter is sticky, grease palms or moisten with cold water.)

Makes approximately 20 matzah balls.
Betayavon! (Hearty Appetite!)

Tanta Tee's:
1/2 teaspoon paprika
1/2 teaspoon ginger
no nutmeg

Tanta Gizella's:
no salt
no pepper
no parsley
no nutmeg
no ginger
no paprika

Tanta Gabi's:
Double the amount of matzah meal or add even more! (These may have to cook for a bit longer than the others.)